# Who's in the Pumpkin?

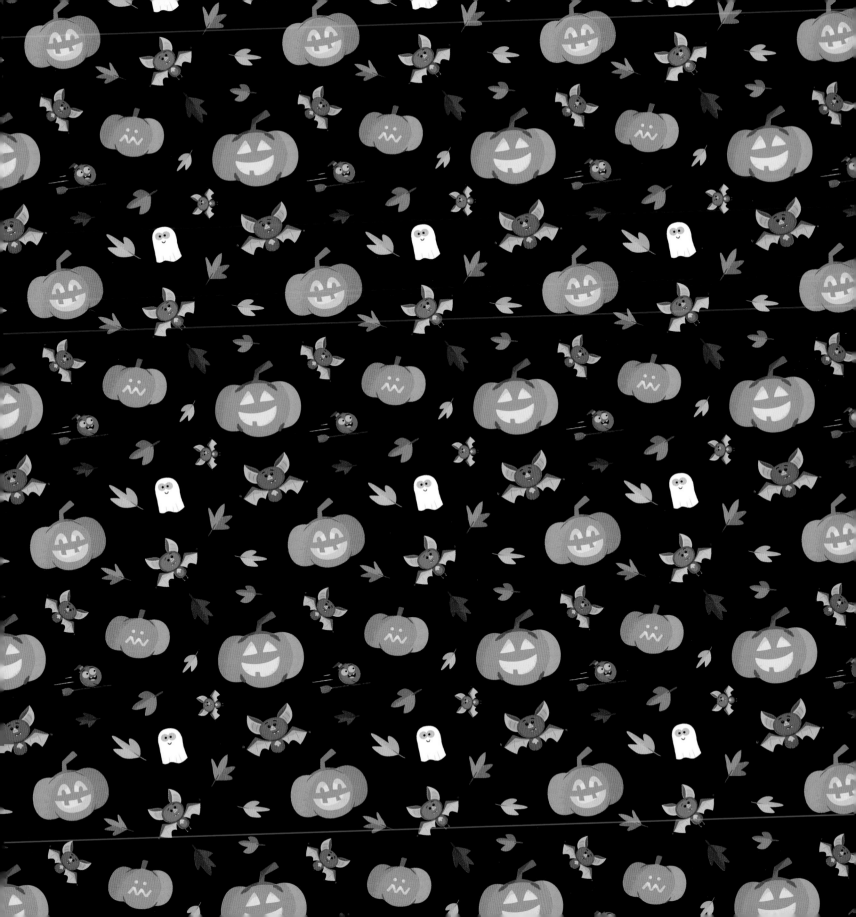

# Can you spot this spider on every page?

First published in Great Britain in 2023 by Pat-a-Cake
Copyright © Hodder & Stoughton Limited 2023. All rights reserved
Pat-a-Cake is a registered trade mark of Hodder & Stoughton Limited

1 3 5 7 9 10 8 6 4 2

Text by Pat-a-Cake · Illustrated by Dean Gray · ISBN: 978 1 52638 399 0
A CIP catalogue record for this book is available from the British Library
Printed and bound in China

Pat-a-Cake, an imprint of Hachette Children's Group
Part of Hodder & Stoughton Limited
Carmelite House, 50 Victoria Embankment, London EC4Y 0DZ
EU address: 8 Castlecourt, Castleknock, Dublin 15, Ireland

An Hachette UK Company
www.hachette.co.uk · www.hachettechildrens.co.uk

# Who's in the Pumpkin?

Illustrated by Dean Gray

It's time for Daddy Ghost to go
trick-or-treating with Baby Ghost,
but he can't find her anywhere!

Is she in the haunted house?

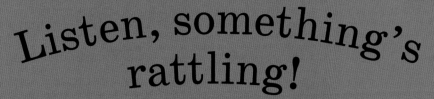

Listen, something's rattling!

Rattle! Rattle!

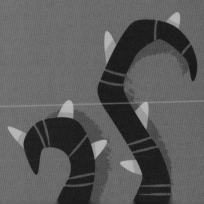

# Who's in the haunted house?

"I'm not Baby Ghost!

I'm a silly skeleton!"

Oh dear, where can Baby Ghost be?

Is she behind the spooky tree?

Listen,
something's
howling!

Awoooo! Awoooo!

# Who's behind the spooky tree?

Daddy Ghost is still looking for Baby Ghost.

Is she in the cauldron?

# Who's in the cauldron?

Where, oh where is Baby Ghost?

Is she behind the creaky door?

# Who's behind the creaky door?

Daddy Ghost has looked EVERYWHERE for Baby Ghost.

Where can she be?

# Who's in the Pumpkin?

"Here I am!
Hello,
Daddy.

Let's go trick-or-treating!"

"Happy Halloween,
Baby Ghost."

"Happy Halloween,
Daddy!"

# There are 15 matching pairs on this page.

# Can you find them all?